Closure

An Upstate Mystery

By FJ Donohue

Closure

Upstate Mystery #2

fj donohue

Published by fj donohue, 2021.

CLOSURE

First edition. May 25, 2021.

ISBN: 979-8215930816

Written by fj donohue.

Also by fj donohue

Endwell Investigations
Full Circle
Vindication

Upstate Mystery
Hit and Run
Two Murders by the River
A Serial Killer Returns
Right Time Wrong Place
The Caribbean Laundry

Upstate Mystery #2
Closure

Upstate Mystery #7
The Snowbird Bank Robber

With thanks to my ever-patient wife Louise and our good friend Judy McMahon for assisting with editing.

Prologue

IT WAS LATE IN THE afternoon on a hot August day in Scranton back in 1975. Sean McCarthy was sitting on his front steps looking out over the street, waiting for his dad to come home from work. They would be playing catch at the park that evening. He noticed a neighborhood kid, Eddie Filmore walking down the street. He was about 4 houses away on the other side. A slick 1975 Pontiac Bonneville 4-door hardtop with a two-tone blue paint job pulled up next to Eddie. The boy started talking with the driver. Then he got in the car. Eddie waved as the car drove by. Eddie was never seen again.

Chapter 1

IT WAS OVER A THREE-hour drive from Binghamton NY to Lancaster PA. Sean needed an early start as he wanted to do this in one day. So, at 6:30 with a toasted bagel and travel mug of coffee, He got on I-81 and headed south from Binghamton. Not a bad day for a drive. Spring had finally settled in and the NY and PA Departments of Transportation had not yet started to repair the roads from the winter limiting the traffic to one or two lanes. Smooth sailing. Sean had to make this trip, if for no other reason than to settle the matter once and for all. He had seen the car in the Scranton Tribune about 4 weeks ago. It had won best car in its class and the article said it would be entered into the upcoming Lancaster antique car show on May 29th. The show was actually at the West Lampeter Fairgrounds, about 7 miles southeast of Lancaster, one of many community fairgrounds in PA. He had to find out. Was this the car?

Having grown up in Scranton, Sean had kept up his connections with his hometown over the years. A subscription to the newspaper was an integral part in maintaining his roots as well as trips to Scranton to visit old friends. His grandfather had come from Ireland and had worked in the coal mines in and around Lackawanna county. It was a hard life in the mines but he supported his family as best he could. He had been proud of his son, Sean's father. He had become a policeman and had risen through the ranks to be a detective.

He made sure Sean and his sister Maggie were educated. Their parents always insisted that sports were secondary to academics. If your grades did not meet their standard for what they expected from you, athletics stopped until you were back on track. The children understood the importance of an education and the support provided by their parents. Maggie was a high school math teacher and coached the girls swim team. Sean was a natural athlete. More than that, he was gifted. His hand eye coordination and timing were excellent. And he was fast. In high school he had played all three sports. Basketball, football and baseball. His first love was football. There was nothing more exciting than coming through the line through between guard and tackle and going up the field. It was you against the defenders.

He had been recruited by a number of universities including Penn State. However, he was a bit small for the size they liked for their halfbacks and Penn State had not offered him a full scholarship. Their loss, University of Maryland's gain. Sean was a starter in his freshman year and was Atlantic Coast Conference first team for the remaining three years. His number was retired in 2005. After graduation, he went to Penn State and earned a masters degree in math, just like his sister. At Penn State he worked for Papa Joe Paterno in the athletic office, did a bit of coaching and tutoring some of the ballplayers. Sean always remembered Papa Joe saying they shouldn't have let him get away.

He was amazed when he'd read about the horrific crimes committed against young boys at Penn State. He was there when this was happening. Why didn't he see any of this? Was he blind? How did this happen? He thought even now if he were to ask a parent to name two places where their children would be safe. He bet the universities and their church would be named. Yet these were the centers of these terrible acts. He vowed that if he ever came across this in his career he would not rest until the criminals were brought to justice.

After getting his graduate degree Sean had gone back to his first love football. He taught high school math and was the assistant coach at Scranton High School and then took over head football coaching duties at Binghamton High School. He stayed 25 years. Now he had decided to retire after next season.

Chapter 2

THE SCRANTON TIMES-Tribune usually arrived by mail two to three days after publication. Sixty miles between Binghamton and Scranton yet 2-3 days by mail. Such is the modern age thought Sean. He could read a digital version but he was more comfortable with a newspaper in hand. He liked the feel of it. Like all the newspapers today, the Times-Tribune was struggling with providing a good local news feed. Not enough money to pay reporters. The whole industry was changing so rapidly.

It was a Saturday morning about four weeks ago. Two editions of the Times-Tribune were on the kitchen table waiting for him. The High School football season was long over and the school year was winding down. He had taught three classes this year. Geometry/Trigonometry, Algebra II and AP math, which meant a heavier dose of calculus. Although most of his problem children were in the Geometry/Trig class, he still enjoyed it the most. Geometry and trig could take you to a place where you defined spatial relationships. Some of them saw that, others didn't, but all told, he had good kids this year.

Now he had time to catch up on the hometown news. He wasn't really concentrating just leafing through the papers looking for something to catch his interest. Mostly just looking at pictures. He was in the local news section of the Thursday paper when a picture jumped out at him.

"Jesus Jenny!" cried Sean, "it can't be!"

"Are you talking to me?" asked Moira. She had just come into the kitchen. "You don't look well at all, is something wrong? You look like you just saw a ghost."

"Well," said Sean, "maybe closer than you think."

"Seriously Sean, you don't look well. What's going on?"

"Do you remember me telling you about the kid on our street back when I was 12 or so who got into a car and was never seen again?"

"Not in any great detail," replied Moira, "but I do remember you and your sister talking about it at a family gathering."

Sean handed her the paper and pointed to the picture. According to the reporter, it was a 1975 Pontiac Bonneville 4 door hardtop. It was in original condition, never restored. Other than the usual repairs like battery, brakes, plugs, tires, etc., the car was an original according to the newspaper. The article said it was a Scranton car and had stayed local.

"That's the car! The one that took Eddie! I'm sure of it!" he said. Sean went through the details of the abduction with Moira. How he was the last guy to see Eddie Filmore and how the police spent a lot of time investigating the abduction but were never able to find the car or the driver. Sean always felt guilty that he had not observed enough detail to help them catch the guy. The police checked with all the Pontiac dealers in and around the Scranton area but could not locate the car. A search of the PA Department of Motor Vehicles records did not turn up anything of value. It was as if a mystery car had come into Scranton, picked up Eddie Filmore and disappeared. Sean could not recall any more information about the car. It had been especially hard on Sean's father. The Filmores were good friends. He had kept the file on Eddie open for years but never got a solid lead. As the years went by it was still a topic of conversation that came up from time to time. Sean knew Eddie's father had died. His mother was still alive and Eddie had two brothers who were still in the Scranton area.

Now he had a terrible feeling in the pit of his stomach and thought he might be sick. He was sure this was the car. Then he thought, was the owner the car he saw in the newspaper connected to Eddie? Was he still around? Sean had no memory of the driver from back in 1975. It was all over so quickly and for a 12year old kid, the car was the main interest. Now, he had to get some answers.

Sean looked at Moira and said again, "The picture in the newspaper! That's the car. I know it, I know it!"

"How can you be sure? It was almost 40 years ago."

"I don't know," said Sean, "but I just know."

"What are you going to do?"

"I'm going to that show in Lancaster and see for myself."

Chapter 3

THE COUNTY FAIRGROUNDS in West Lampeter provided a good venue for the antique car show. The grounds were ample for displaying the cars and the location was a good draw for Maryland and southern PA. It was a cloudy day but no rain was in the forecast. A good day to walk around and see the cars. There was quite a range: Thunderbirds, Corvettes, some hot rods, Model T's and A's, vintage sports cars and a surprising assembly of production cars that had survived over the years. Sean was surprised at the number and variety of them. The field was organized according to type and class. The show promoter provided a guide for the categories and locations of the cars.

There were about 10 Pontiacs displayed. GTO's, Le Mans, even a Safari station wagon. The 1975 Bonneville was at the end of the line. Sean could not see anyone around the car, so he had a good opportunity to check it out without someone looking over his shoulder. He looked at it from all sides and then concentrated on the passenger side as that was what he remembered going past him. It took him back in time. He started to sweat and he wondered if he was going to hyperventilate.

Go slow, he told himself, *look with your eyes and not your emotions.*

"Can I tell you anything about the car?" asked a man coming up to him.

Sean said, "They only made that side view mirror for the Bonneville in 1975."

"You know your cars, my friend, most folks would never pick up on that except the judges."

Sean replied, "I loved cars as a kid, studied all I could about them from magazines mostly."

"Me too, fell in love with them and never looked back."

Clearly the car's years did not fit with the guy's age. The guy looked to be over forty but too young to be the driver of the car from the day. Maybe his father, other member of the family or clan owned the car back in 1975? Sean decided to keep the conversation going and see where it led.

"This is a rude question but if I may," asked Sean, "is there any money in showing these cars at the various shows? I saw you won a prize in Scranton the other week."

"Not really. You do it mostly for the social scene, also win a few trophies. You can sell the car and maybe move on to something better. My name is Carl by the way. I'm a Scranton guy."

"I grew up in Scranton, live in Binghamton now," said Sean.

Okay thought Sean, time to move onto the real questions. "How long have you owned the car?"

"Maybe 6 years or so now," replied Carl. "Bought it off a guy at one of these shows. He had three other antique cars and his wife wanted the stable downsized. I always liked the lines of this model and this one has survived quite well over the years. It has very few miles on it. I trailer it to the shows to keep the miles down. It is really important with older production cars. First question a prospective buyer asks is, what are the miles on it?"

Sean was between a rock and a hard place now. He felt he could not tell Carl that he thought his car may have been involved in an abduction 40 years ago, it might shut down any cooperation from him. But he did not want to tell him a lie or deceive him. He was walking a fine line as Carl was his only source of information at this point. *Well,* he thought, *I guess I can start by telling him it may have been involved in a crime that was never solved. If Carl wants to go deeper, then I'll tell him the whole story.*

With a bit of apprehension, Sean started out, "I'm trying to trace this car back to the original owner. I believe I saw it back in 1975 and it may have been involved in a crime which was never solved."

"Whoa, that's quite a challenge," said Carl, "what was it, a get-away car in a bank robbery?"

"Far from it, it may have been part of a child abduction."

"Are you kidding me!"

"No, I'm not," said Sean. "I was 12 years old at the time and saw the car pick up a neighborhood kid and drive away, they never found the kid or the car."

Carl asked, "Never seen again, the kid or the car?"

"Yup, the kid's name was Eddie Filmore."

"How do you know it was this car?" asked Carl.

"Well I really don't," said Sean, "but when I saw the picture in the Scranton Times Tribune, I just had this feeling that after all these years, it was back and I need to find some closure. My father was a Scranton police detective in those days. He tried to close the case but never could get a break. He kept Eddie's file open for the rest of his working days and into retirement. Even after all those years he didn't forget it. I know I am asking a lot but without your cooperation, I can't try to sort this out."

"I know this car has been through a number of owners over the years," replied Carl, "but I'm happy to give you whatever help I can. It may be impossible to trace, but if you want to try, I'll do whatever I can."

Well thought Sean, a good starting point and God love him, the guy had stepped up. Carl was approached by another person asking questions about the car, so Sean took the time to look over the car again. He had only seen one side of it in 1975 but now he took the time to looked it all over inside and out. He took a series of pictures with his phone and would upload them to his computer when he got home. There weren't any distinguishing marks on the car that Sean could remember, so he finished up by just looking at the passenger side of the car and wondering if this was it? Am I missing anything? The only thing he did remember was what he had told Carl about the side view mirrors being unique to the 1975 Bonneville year. It changed in 1976, so he knew that this car fit the specific year.

Carl came back over to Sean. "It always happens," he said, "the guy I was talking to told me his father had this model Pontiac. Lots of the visitors to these shows love to go down memory lane. Okay Sean, where do you want to start in your search?"

"Let's check the VIN and see what that can tell us," offered Sean.

"Sure, we can do that, but you need to understand that although Vehicle Identification Numbers were started back in 1955, which is good news, they were not standardized back then. So, it's hit or miss on the information you can obtain. The car guys pretty much put in whatever they thought was important to them at the time. There wasn't any uniformity until 1981 when the DOT set up a protocol for the VINs. If the original owner sold the car before 1981, the VIN records may be thin. Also, most of these cars are private sales so the VIN numbers are not of much interest to the buyers if the cars aren't registered. It could be on the subsequent sales information, but don't count on it."

"Then I'm at a dead end already?" asked Sean.

"Not necessarily," said Carl. "You need to think about multiple sources for information and see what you can put together. The VIN history after 1981 could be helpful in tracing a history line but you need to know that a lot of these cars are sold and never registered. They're trailered from show to show. They are road capable but the owners don't want to subject them to the wear and tear. As I said that's what I'm doing now with the Bonneville."

"Okay, I'll start there, any other things I should be looking at?"

Carl said, "You can try and trace the license plates back and see how far you can go with them. I don't want to give you any false hopes. The Department of Motor Vehicles records are sketchy. The early ones were all on paper for years and stored in different places. Harrisburg, counties, cities, you name it. When they converted to a digital format, most of the older records were probably destroyed. My thinking is you won't have a clear trail. You'll need to paste together a lot of information and get lucky."

"Thanks, I really appreciate your interest and perspective."

"Let's do this," Carl said, "copy down the current plate number and VIN. I'll give you my cell phone number and email. Keep in touch and maybe I can help you along the way. Let me have your contact info also."

On the way back, Sean's head was swimming with all kinds of thoughts. This is so complex, too long ago, multiple owners and no clear path forward. He was so engrossed in thinking of all the issues, he didn't have any clear memory of the drive back and only "awoke" when he pulled into his driveway in Binghamton.

Chapter 4

WHEN SEAN CAME INTO the house, Moira was just finishing up some gardening work in the backyard. She always joked about making sure the rabbits, squirrels and chipmunks had enough to eat. It was a constant challenge with the squirrels. They were so clever and could get into everything so easily.

"How did it go Sean? I hope you weren't disappointed."

"Perplexed is more like it," said Sean. "I did see the car and Carl, the owner, was very helpful. It's just not a straight line to the answer. The car has had multiple owners and records are a real problem. I don't know if I can ever sort it out. I may have a solid gut feeling about the car but not sure I can prove it. And, even if I can, so much time has passed by, what will it all prove? Everyone is probably dead, most likely Eddie too. I don't really know where to begin."

"Sounds to me like a typical start of football season," said Moira. "Make a list, set priorities and work them down. Maybe you can't get there but at least someone has tried, yet again, to find Eddie Filmore."

"You're right Moira. I'm getting swallowed up by the problem. I need to take a step back and maybe put some outside eyes on it."

"Talk to Junior Roberts. He's practical and you guys always got along well. I know you respect him. Both of you approach coaching the same way in terms of team play. He would be a good sounding board."

"I'll talk to him. I have to go over to the office tomorrow and I'm pretty sure he'll be there."

"Sean, there may never be closure for Eddie. It's been a long, long time. Do the best you can. What do you always tell your players?"

"Oh yeah, play hard."

The two coaches had adjacent offices just off the gym. Junior had been coaching the men's basketball team at Binghamton High for about 8 years. He had a good won/lost record and his players bought into his style and program. He was all about the team and developing players. All teams have a culture fostered by the coach. Some were good coaches committed to their players and others were only there for their ego. Actually this was a busy time for Junior. He coached AAU (Amateur Athletic Union) basketball in the summer. The Binghamton area team called the "Storm" looked good this year with senior players and some "newbies" coming along showing good promise. Junior liked the AAU season as it gave him a chance to look over the local and area talent. It gave him a preview of what he would be up against next season.

Junior was in his office setting up the practice schedule. His players were in the gym warming up, taking shots and playing horse. Lots of chatter and laughing. *Looks like good chemistry,* thought Junior. The coach came out of his office and called the players to a circle.

"Okay guys, this is our first time together so let's set the rules of engagement. This is a short season, seven weeks, and very intense. We play at least one game every week. We practice two times a week. You practice, you play. I don't want any "contractors" on the team. No individual players. Yes, I said team and that is what we are going to work to develop. We play team ball and we play for each other. We all play at different levels, I get that, but when we play as a team we are all at a higher level. Rahim, you are probably the best player on our team and a senior. I'm looking to you and the other seniors to provide leadership. Team leadership."

"I understand coach," Rahim said, "We'll be there."

"I know you guys will, thanks."

Today was more administration than practice. Junior reviewed the schedule and went over the practice times and game locations. He handed out the basketball jerseys: black on one side, white on the other with a contrasting color for the team name and number.

There was a lot of discussion and negotiation, if you can call it that, between the players over who got what number.

Everyone wanted the number of their favorite NBA player. Junior always loved the banter between the guys as they tried to seal the deal for the number they wanted. Jaime Prono was a new player this season and happy for any number. He was more interested in fitting in with the team. Jaime was clearly a work in progress, a gangly kid growing in all directions. Junior really liked his basic skills. Stuff you cannot really teach. Jaime never got lost on the court, had good hand-eye coordination and a great sense of ball movement. He could be an impact player in a couple of years.

In the stands was a younger lad, not yet in high school but looking on. Gary Hagan was always with Jaime. After the tragic events in his life, the murder of his father, and his mother being implicated in the crime, he had more or less been adopted by Jaime. The two boys were like brothers. Gary was playing CYO (Catholic Youth Organization) basketball in the fall. Junior planned to keep an eye on him for the future.

After practice Junior came back to his office to finish up some paperwork.

"Junior, do you have a few minutes to talk?" asked Sean.

"Sure coach," Junior said, "as long as you are not going to give me your secret pick and roll play again!"

"Promise I won't."

"Okay. As my daughter says: Sup?"

Brad replied, "You don't remember this as it was back in 1975 in Scranton before your time. I was 12 years old then. It was a summer afternoon and I was sitting on my front steps. A really nice car came down the street and slowed down by a younger kid who lived 4 houses down from me. His name was Eddie Filmore by the way. Anyway, Eddie got into the car, it drove off and nobody ever saw Eddie again. They never found the boy or the car."

"Oh, wow" said Junior. "That's awful!"

Sean continued. "You know I still get the Times-Tribune sent up from Scranton."

"I sure do, I've seen them in your office over the years."

Sean nodded. "When I was looking through the newspapers the other day, I saw a picture of a guy and his car. He had just won one of those best in class awards at a local antique car show. The car was a 1975 Pontiac Bonneville 4 door hardtop. The picture was in color and it was the car that took Eddie Filmore away!"

Junior looked taken aback. "That's a bit of a stretch don't you think?" he said. "How can you be sure? Did it have any special markings? Was the guy in the paper the same one from 1975? Do you have any tangible proof?"

"I just know, it's the car. It's had multiple owners over the years. But, I've got this feeling in my gut and I know that for whatever reason, this is the car and I have to find the original owner. Junior, I can't let this go, I have to go wherever this leads me. Eddie's mom is still alive and he has two brothers who are also alive. I have to try to sort this out."

"Okay, I understand, at least I think I do, but you can't do this by yourself. You need help from someone who knows where to look and how to go about it. Without this kind of help, you'll end up chasing your tail and just get frustrated."

"Are you suggesting I hire a private investigator?"

"No, but you'll need someone who has done this kind of work who can help you out and give you direction," said Junior. "Look, I've got this kid on my AAU team, Jaime Prono. His dad, Spud, works for the District Attorney as an investigator. He has a friend who was a detective and also worked in the DA's office as an investigator. He was the guy who solved the murder of Jake Hagan on Colesville road about 1 ½ years ago. His name is Brad Petronella. He is retired now and does volunteer mediation work at the Resolution Center and assignments for the District Attorney in town. I know Spud. We met a few times regarding Jaime. If you like, we can talk with Spud and see what he thinks. Maybe ask him to talk to Brad about helping you.

"Do you think he'll help?" asked Sean.

"Who knows? If you don't go fishing, you ain't gonna catch anything!"

Chapter 5

IT WAS A WARM, SUNNY afternoon about a week later when they met up with Brad Petronella, the investigator Junior had talked about. They sat out on the deck at Brad's place. Jaime Prono and Gary Hagan were in the driveway along with two other kids playing half court two on two. Lots of laughing and trash talk. Jaime was playing on what he considered his home court as Brad had kept the court in good playing shape after his kids had left the nest. The neighborhood kids had taken it over. He loved to see them out in the driveway. Jaime knew every crack and bump in the driveway. He was a handful to guard. But the kid guarding him was pretty good. He played right in Jaime's face, not giving him any open space. Twenty points to a game and then they switched players. Jaime and the other kids were older and more experienced than Gary so he was getting a great tutorial. Half court games were different than playing on a full court as the space is tight especially in a driveway. This was a challenge for Gary, but he was stepping up, not intimidated by the older guys.

There was the usual small talk between the men about the football and basketball teams and what the upcoming seasons might look like. Both Sean and Junior were optimistic about their teams' chances. But, until you have a couple of games under your belt, you really don't know. Junior had good words about Jaime, both his attitude and development.

"Spud told me you were trying to find the original owner of a car from 1975," said Brad. "Can you give me some background?"

Sean spent the next fifteen minutes reviewing all the details of Eddie Filmore's abduction and how the case was never solved. He told Brad about seeing the picture in the newspaper and how it had affected him. He saw Spud and Brad glance at each other when he got to that part.

"I know you think I am crazy," said Sean, "but I know in my heart that this is the car. I have never had a feeling like this before. It's the car, I just know it."

"Okay let's not get ahead of ourselves," replied Brad. If you want to do this, you have to let the evidence lead the investigation, not your emotions. Consistent, pragmatic investigation is the mantra."

"I don't have the background, experience, or skills to do this," said Sean. "I'm going to need help. I am not even sure where to start at this point. I have pictures of the car plus the VIN for what it is worth, it's from 1975. And the current owner is willing to help where he can."

"Well that's not a bad start," Spud said. "What do you think Brad?"

"Yeah, it's a good start," said Brad. "The current owner may be your best source at the beginning as he knows the antique car business. I can see you going back to him again. The main challenge now is to get access to all the records you can on the car. DMV and VIN stuff. I think they will be all over the place. Cities, counties, Harrisburg. You are looking at 40 years of records and also a conversion to a digital process at some point which means a lot of the old data may be lost or was never digitized."

"Let me be right up front with you," Sean said. "Can you help me?"

"I think I can," replied Brad. "I volunteer at the Resolution Center in town and occasional work for the DA, mostly reviewing cases before they go to the Grand Jury. I just finished some work for the DA and don't see anything coming right away. So, yes I can help but we need to be realistic."

"What do you mean?" asked Sean.

"We have to put this investigation on a clock." explained Brad. "You'll be on Summer break pretty soon. But in the Fall, your busy days start and will run for at least 3 months. Maybe longer if you have a good team and go to the state playoffs. My sense is that if we can't solve the case by the Fall, given the demands on your time and frankly mine also, we may not be able to do it. So, we have a window of opportunity."

"I'll take it," said Sean, "thank you."

"We're going to need a lot of help from the folks at the state capitol in Harrisburg," said Brad. "We need an entry to a lot of city and county offices looking for records. A lot of times these offices don't want to take the time to open the doors so to speak. Too many other things going on."

Junior jumped up and almost fell off the deck, "Sean, isn't that great kid you had about 15 years ago a prosecutor now with the Attorney General in Harrisburg?"

"You mean Tommy Reynolds?" replied Sean.

Junior said, "Yeah, that's him!"

Tommy, oh yes! Tommy Reynolds. In a coaching career, a kid like that comes along once if you're lucky. It may even happen twice if you are really, really lucky. This happened to Sean. But Tommy was the first and they had formed a bond that was still in place today. They kept in touch over the years and especially during football season. Sean also followed Tommy's career in Harrisburg.

He first met Tommy when he was a freshman trying out for the team. He had elected to try out as a defensive player, safety, because he was just a freshman and there were a lot of seniors on the team. Sean noticed that nobody got by Tommy. He was quick and read the plays well. He still remembered one play during practice when their star running back, Paul Paquette, ran the ball. Paul was called "the steam roller" by his teammates. He was a little under 5'8" and built like a fire hydrant. If he got through the line into the backfield he was very hard to defend. On this particular play, Paul hit the backfield at full speed. Tommy came up, challenged him and took him down right at the ankles. A textbook tackle. Paul was down in a heartbeat and got up ever so slowly.

But what really got Sean's attention was the way Tommy could throw a football. Most high school players typically throw the football like a baseball. Big arm movements, almost like baseball windups sometimes. A slow release easy to see and defend. Tommy threw the ball like the NFL quarterbacks. Short take back just behind the head and quick release. Sean asked Tommy where he learned to do that and he told him that his father taught him how to throw. He would have him stand with his back against a wall and throw the ball. They always watched the NFL games and he and his dad would talk about different players and their styles.

Tommy was moved over to backup quarterback and soon was the starting quarterback. A senior, who had the job at the time, was hurt in an early game and out for the season. So, the transition to Tommy was not a big setback for the senior. From there, Tommy went from strength to strength. In his senior year all the big schools came calling. He could have gone anywhere he wanted. He could have been another Joe Namath from Beaver Falls PA who played at Alabama. But Tommy's horizon was far ahead of college football. He wanted a career after athletics.

Sean and Tommy had talked about it. In Tommy's mind it was quite logical. He loved upstate NY and PA and wanted to be a lawyer. So, he played football at Syracuse on a full scholarship. Syracuse understood his long-term goals and committed to a quality undergraduate education. During the season it was difficult to maintain a consistent class schedule with all the demands of practice and travel to away games. Summer school filled in the missed classes and lab work. He majored in Economics and minored in math. After graduation, he played 8 years in the NFL with the Patriots and Eagles. He never made it to the big game but he was in 3 playoffs. Off season he got a law degree from Syracuse which was part of the original commitment from the university. It took over 7 years but he met his goal. He passed the bar in NY, PA and MA in short order. After that, he left the NFL to follow his real passion, the law. He could have played more seasons in the NFL but did not want to put his future at risk. This was long before the exposure of the head injury problems. However, the players knew something was not right even if the NFL was in total denial.

From there Tommy went to work with the Attorney General in Harrisburg where he stayed. He was now the lead prosecutor, had married and was raising a family. He had been approached to run for Attorney General but did not want to play on the political side of the job.

"I'll call Tommy and see if he can run interference for us with the various agencies. A call from the AG's office should make things move," said Sean.

"Is that legal?" asked Junior.

'I believe so," replied Brad. "Just make sure you're up front with him on the case and what we want him to do. We don't want any legwork from his office without his approval. We'll need some supporting calls, research and maybe some advice along the way. Don't forget, this is a potential murder case."

"Understood, I'll call him tomorrow," said Sean.

Chapter 6

SEAN CALLED TOMMY THE next day.

"Coach! so nice to hear from you. How is life in the coaching world? Going to the state finals this year?"

"Always hoping," said Sean, "if you come back for one more season, we should make it. How is everyone doing? Kids driving you crazy?"

"Ruth is fine and my girls are the best. Love being a dad even though they don't listen to me anymore."

"Just talk louder. Works every time." said Sean.

"You're a lifesaver, Coach! Always good advice! So, what can I do for you?"

"Do you have a few minutes to listen to a rather strange story and request?" asked Sean.

"Sure, fire away."

Sean went through all the history about Eddie Filmore and continued up to his trip to the antique auto show and the meeting with Junior, Spud and Brad. The story kept growing and Sean was a bit worried that he would miss some important parts. But it seemed to hold together and Tommy did not ask for many clarifications. When he finished there was a long silence on the line.

"You think I'm crazy?" asked Sean.

"No not at all, coach," replied Tommy, "I'm a bit taken back that you are carrying this load. You would think after forty plus years, it would be more historical than emotional."

"I know, Tommy. The picture just put me in another place and I have to find out for sure if the guy who took Eddie was the owner of that car.

Eddie was 8 years old and then gone, most likely dead. I want to try and find some closure."

"What do you want me to do, or more importantly, what do you want from this office?" said Tommy.

"My main worry is that when we start calling the various local and county offices looking for information, they'll just blow us off. Same with your headquarters in Harrisburg and even the Feds if we need to look there. My thought is that a call from your office would provide the incentive to cooperate. I'm not looking for any "boots on the ground" Tommy, just the leverage you guys can provide to open some doors for us. I've met with a retired investigator from the Broome County District Attorney's office. His name is Brad Petronella. I think he's pretty good and he said he would help."

Tommy replied, "I know Mary Louise Eldridge, the DA there, and she's mentioned him. I've also heard of him from some of the cops in Binghamton. He was a detective at one time. Okay I think I understand what you're looking for. Let me talk to the boss and get back to you. I've an intern for the summer who is a real hawk. She's the best detail person I've seen in some time. This could be a great introduction for her to learn about the various levels of government around the state. I'll have her on other assignments too but this could be a great learning experience and she will meet a lot of new people. Give me a day or so. The boss is out of town but will be back the day after tomorrow."

"You're the mailman Tommy, you always deliver," said Sean

"That was Karl Malone of the Utah Jazz, coach, but it does sound good!"

Sean did not want to tie up any more of Tommy's busy day so after a few more of "how goes it" he rang off. He then called Brad and Spud to let them know about the conversation. Brad was happy with these first steps. They would need some horsepower to move forward in a timely manner. Nothing like a call from the Attorney General's office to get your attention.

Brad said, "Let's not wait for the phone to ring. Assume that Tommy will get this approved and we can forward. In the meantime, go online and run the VIN you took off the car in Lampeter and see what you can find. Maybe a trail, most likely twists and turns, but I don't want you sitting around. Also see if you can find out how many of the models were built and maybe get a geographical fix on them and possibly some info on colors. What was the most popular one, etc. Any information has value at this point."

Sean felt as if a load had been taken off his shoulders. Finally, he was on the hunt and the act of doing something was a source of energy for him. Final exams were next week and then he was off for the Summer so he could put all his energies into this. He was comfortable working with Brad. He did not have an agenda and his approach to the problem was realistic. Sean knew he could not do this by himself. Also, when Brad put a clock on the effort it was very clear he had to focus on the problem and spend his time wisely. He would avoid the dead ends. He told himself not to wear out his welcome with Brad. Don't pester him too much.

When Sean got home he sat down with Moira to fill her in on the developments.

"How is your third son?", his wife asked. "You and the boys are so close to Tommy he's really part of our family."

"Sure is." said Sean, "As soon as he answered the phone, the time just turned back and it is as if we never were apart. He's doing well, as are Ruth and the girls. I think he will be able to help me through his office. I told him I have a really good feeling about Brad Petronella. Junior was great putting me with him."

Okay Sean thought, time to get on the internet and see what is going on with VIN numbers. Fortunately, there were all kinds of apps dealing with VIN numbers: one to check the car you are thinking of buying, one to check on the car you should have bought and one to check on the car you are glad you didn't buy! However, given the manufacture date was 1975, and hadn't been on the road in recent years, it was not going to be very easy to find any definitive information. But he was able to find the VIN number for a few years beginning in 1985 so it appeared to him that the car was in fact registered and had been driven at various times. He also found it listed in 1996 and guessed that was the guy who had sold it to Carl around 2016. Carl never put the car on the road, so he did not register it with the DMV. Sean made a note to check the name with Carl and see if he could find an address for the guy. The VIN listing for 1985 meant it was registered and on the road then. Need to find that guy also. But this line of investigation was drying up quickly, so Sean started researching the Bonneville model while waiting for Tommy to come back to him. He made a list of the action items from his limited VIN and model search. He would get with Brad to review the material.

What else? Sean had noted that the show in Lampeter was very well organized and the cars were grouped according to their pedigree. So, he wondered, are there any clubs or organizations these guys belong to who might have records of cars, member names and maybe even sales? Carl would know, he had been an antique car collector for years.

"Carl? This is Sean McCarthy, remember me?"

"Sure I do," said Carl, "how goes the hunt?"

"Just getting started," said Sean, "and I can see it isn't gonna be easy. I am trying to find a track to follow that may lead to something and so far all I can see are the problems."

"You said you were just getting started," replied Carl, "you don't hit a homerun every time at bat or, in your case, score a touchdown on every possession. You have to move the ball down the field."

"That's a great analogy Carl! I 'm going to use that with my team this Fall. Kids these days seem to be looking for instant gratification. Moving the ball down the field to get into position to score says it all!"

"I'm sure you didn't call me for a motivational speech," said Carl, "how can I help?"

Sean asked, "are there clubs or organizations specific to antique cars and are there regional and national groups?"

"Yes to all," said Carl, "I belong to a number of them. There is a very good national organization and they publish a monthly magazine. Then there's a northeast organization and even one for PA. The northeast and PA organization's value is mainly in show listings and sales of vehicles. Sometimes good stuff on restoration techniques and projects too."

"Are they on line?" asked Sean.

"In the past few years, they've been going more and more digital. The stuff from earlier years is usually whatever magazines are stored in someone's garage or attic. I've copies of the PA and Northeast organization that I've kept over the years. By no means complete but quite a bit of stuff. Also, I donated my monthly national organization magazines to the library here in Scranton. I am not sure what branch actually has the mags but that's easy to find out. If you want, you can come down here and I'll give you what I have and you can also go to the library and look through their magazines."

"Day after tomorrow?" asked Sean.

"That will work, you have my address."

Sean thought it best he check in with Brad to update him on his efforts to date. Brad was quite happy with what Sean had done as It showed he was invested in the problem and was not just looking to him to sort it out.

"I think it's a good idea to go and gather up all of Carl's club stuff and also see if you can find those national organization magazines at the library," replied Brad. "I'm doing a mediation now and I think it will be a two-day affair. After that I can spend some time with you and we can see where we are so far."

"I found the library that has the magazines." said Sean. "It's a branch of the main library, called the Nancy K. Holmes. I called and they have them and were sort of happy to have someone interested in looking at them."

"I see the national magazine more as background information but a good thing to have. Maybe the regional and state stuff Carl has will be helpful, to us "intrepid investigators", assuming he has more than a couple of copies."

Chapter 7

TWO DAYS LATER, SEAN was on I-81S headed to Carl's place and then the library. Carl lived in Clarks Summit, north of Scranton, just off I-81S. It was an easy connection for Sean. Carl was in his garage working on a two door 1947 Ford sedan.

"Just picked this up a couple of weeks ago," he said after shaking Sean's hand. "Not in bad shape. My dad had one just like this so I feel as if I am doing work for the family. Dad bought his in 1950 and traded it in around 1955. He bought a new 4 door light blue Ford Customline."

"Did the '47 Ford cost a lot?" asked Sean.

"About $6,000," said Carl. "I'll need to take out the engine, transmission and clutch and get them rebuilt. The inside is in pretty good shape, even has the original radio. The rust issues are manageable, so all in, a good car to restore."

He gave Sean three large boxes of PA and Northeast club magazines. He hadn't expected so much material. There could be something here he thought. Or maybe the problem was going to be too much information and he would spend the summer researching clubs and cars without any results. Okay he reminded himself, don't get ahead of the evidence. He also thought about Carl's football analogy. Move the ball, move the ball.

"My wife is really happy to see this stuff move out of the house, Sean," Carl said, "she keeps asking me to clean it up. No rush on bringing it back!"

"Quick question Carl." Sean said after putting the boxes in the trunk.

"Sure, what is it?"

"In looking at VINS, I found one from 2010. Was that the year you bought the car?" asked Sean.

"Nope, bought it in 2012 from a guy named Fred Pelletier. Not surprised he had it for such a short time. He had 3 other cars and as I may have mentioned, his wife was getting fed up with all the cars at the house. He told me she said the place looked like a used car lot. That happens a lot with collectors. One car then two and on from there.

Sean chatted with Carl a bit more about the antique car game and then headed out to the Nancy K. Holmes library. The librarian was happy to see him. Probably they didn't get much call for the magazines. More likely he was the first person who had ever been interested. They were all organized on a storage shelf in the basement by year and month. There were reading desks in the storage room which the librarian called "the stacks". She told him if he wanted, he could take copies with him. It was not their policy to lend out material from the reference stacks but as nobody had ever asked for the magazines in over twenty years, she was only too pleased!

H'm thought Sean, start in the front or back years? He was standing closer to the current years so the decision was made. He spent the remainder of the morning, the afternoon and into the evening reviewing the magazines a pile at a time. The library closed at 8 PM and then he was on his way back to Binghamton with three boxes from Carl and 20 national magazines with some information of interest.

When he got home, there was a voice message from Tommy Reynolds telling him that the AG's office would support him, and he had assigned their intern Theresa Marcheto as the point person for the task. Sean copied down Theresa's email and phone number. The next day, he met with Brad at the Resolution Center, where he was finishing up some paperwork from an earlier mediation. The center was ideal for a quiet, private place to talk. Sean first explained what he had found out about the VIN numbers. They knew it was a long shot given the relatively recent requirement for the Federal protocols for the VIN numbers and how, even now, they might be missing from the records if a car is only sold and not registered. In fact, Sean had only a few dates where the car's VIN number showed up. Pretty thin at this point. But since a few did show up, it was most likely that the car had been registered with the DMV and had names associated with it. Brad told him to pass that information to Theresa at the AG's office and see what she could find in terms of names at the DMV. 1996 and 2010 should be manageable, but 1985 was a hope and a prayer. That was probably right in the middle of the digital revolution. Brad also told Sean to make sure he copied Tommy Reynolds on all the activity with the AG's office. He did not want to do anything outside of their channels. The AG was doing them a favor and he did not want to push it.

"Why wouldn't the VIN at least show up on the initial purchase of the car in 1975?" asked Sean.

"Maybe it did but the record is lost. Maybe it was from another state and in those days there wasn't any consistency in Federal record keeping," said Brad. "All we know is it's not there now. So, let's work with the information we have. I want to see what we can get from the DMV records and find out where they keep them. Can you ask Theresa to look into that also? I am not clear on who we need to talk to so let's start with the big dogs in Harrisburg."

Sean called Theresa Marcheto at the AG's office that afternoon. He introduced himself and filled her in on his investigations so far.

"Please call me Terry," she said at once. "Tommy says to call you Coach. He said if I call you Mr. McCarthy, you may not take my calls!"

"Coach is great Terry. Gotta love Tommy. I see that he has you calling him by his preferred name."

"I started out calling him sir and Mr. Reynolds but he said we needed to change that and get on familiar ground as colleagues. It was a bit strange at first but everyone in the office calls him Tommy, even the cafeteria staff and security guards. Imagine that, the lead prosecutor! This is a great place to learn. I am so lucky to have this job, there were a zillion applicants, many from big name schools. But he called me at home after the interview and said you got the job if you want it. Long hours but when you finish, professionally, you will be in a different place."

"He was probably the best player I ever coached," replied Sean. "For a coach, these guys come along once or twice in your career if you are lucky. Sean was my best guy; I am so lucky too. He has a great work ethic and clearly took it to Harrisburg."

"Where do you want to start?" Terry asked.

"The investigator I am working with in Binghamton wants to see what names we can put with the VIN number of an antique Pontiac Bonneville manufactured in 1975. I'm texting you the number and description of the car. We believe it was involved in an abduction and probably murder. I found the VIN number on records for the years 1985, 1996, and 2010. I would like to put names with those dates and any other dates you might find. We need to know what information the DMV has for those VIN numbers and where the information is stored. It gets complicated as there may not be any DMV records if the car was not put on the road. In recent years, it may have just been trailered to antique shows. The other resource is the antique car club material I got from the current owner of the car; a guy named Carl. I'm going to review it over the weekend."

"Okay," said Terry, "I'll get going with my stuff and get back to you shortly. You're looking for names, dates and a timeline for the car, right?"

"You got it Terry," said Sean, "keep in touch."

Sean and Brad divided up the material from Carl and would spent the weekend and maybe the first few days of the following week pouring over it. The national association did not offer much. Brad was hoping for a story about the car which would give them a lead on the original owner. The stories were well written, but the Bonneville was not in any of them. The national magazine was essentially a west coast publication, so the stories were pretty much west of the Mississippi. There were ads for car sales in the back but they were mostly for the very old, expensive cars.

Next up was the northeast regional organization. They produced a magazine every other month containing car stories and cars for sale. Sean got lucky. In 2001 their Bonneville was featured in a story about production cars moving into the antique market and what was important as you hit the 25-year point. The focus of the story were things like original equipment, mileage, the interior and the dreaded rust factor. The Bonneville hit all the markers and was presented as a good example of an emerging antique car. George Winslow of Wilkes Barre was the owner. A long way from 1975 but it was a start. He quickly sent Terry an Email asking her to try and run down (no pun intended) the guy. Sean thought that the PA organization might offer the best source of information. The publication, also published every other month, was mainly a listing of upcoming shows and a comprehensive listing of cars for sale. Maybe he could get closer to 1975.

Chapter 8

THE BIG PUSH WAS TO go through the stuff from Carl.

"Moira, will you help me review the magazines over the weekend?" asked Sean.

"Sure, does this make me a junior investigator?"

"It sure does, and we'll give you a special badge!"

"Oh joy!" replied Moira.

Moira and Sean spread the magazines out on the dining room table, little used these days as the kids were grown and launched. The PA antique car organization was surprisingly well organized. It listed lots of shows throughout the state and a large listing of cars for sale but was very light on feature articles. At this point it did not seem to matter unless he could find one that talked about their car's history from 1975. No such luck. By 10PM Sunday night they had finished their review for Sean's status meeting with Brad on Monday.

Sean met up with Brad at the Resolution Center the next day.

"Okay Sean, talk to me," Brad said. "I know this side of the investigation is tedious but necessary."

"I have some information, but I just don't seem to be able to get back to 1975."

"Show me what you have and let's lay it out on a white board. It will be easier to understand."

Sean went to the white board and started listing what he had:

VIN from 1985

Magazine article from 2001 about the car and its owner, George Winslow of Wilkes Barre.

VIN from 1996

VIN from 2010

Terry at the AG's office is trying to put names with them.

"The fact that the VIN shows up in those years," Sean said, "probably means that the car was registered and on the road. We may be able to get an owner's name. But I can't get earlier than 1985. What happened between 1975 and 1985? Terry is looking at DMV records around the state to see what they've got on file. She asked us to call her when we got through.

"Let's call her then," said Brad.

They called Terry in Harrisburg to see what she had found out.

"Good morning gentlemen," she said. "How is the Binghamton part of the investigation team doing?"

"Waiting for you to save our life!" laughed Sean. "It's the 4th quarter and we're down two touchdowns."

"Just bring in Tommy," she said. "He can do it, Coach! I do have some information for you. I found a DMV record for 1985 and a name. I also have one for 2010 and a name. I think your friend Carl can cover the later years anyway."

"Wow! this is great," said Sean. "But what happened to the DMV records for the other years?"

"That's where it gets dodgy and I think you know what's coming," replied Terry. It's only in the past 15 years or so that the DMV went digital and captured the records. Back in the day, the records were kept at the individual offices in cities, towns and villages. They were supposed to be sent to Harrisburg for filing but it did not always happen. Then when PA made a big push to modernize, not all the records were sent to Harrisburg and those that we sent were not always in the best of shape for transfer to digital media. Clarity, spelling, deterioration of the paper, you name it. I'm still trying to run the Bonneville VIN in the local municipalities. We may get lucky but don't bet a paycheck on it. One of the clerks in the office told me Scranton and some areas around there were "serial offenders". Good old boys with a state job and an attitude."

"Thanks Terry," said Brad, "stay with it if you would. We may get lucky but I think the early stuff is long gone."

"Agreed," said Terry, "now there's another side to this that we need to chase. Given the 1985 and 1996 dates, these guys could be looking at daisies from the roots. So, I'm checking death records and next of kin. As I said I was not able to find any more information on George Winslow from Wilkes Barre. He probably moved out of the area. I could not find a death certificate.

"That's a good point Terry," said Brad. "These guys may be available to us in name only. By the way, I don't want to have you spending your life on this stuff at the expense of solid litigation experience with Tommy. If you think this is more time consuming than initially planned, please let me know. I don't want to take advantage of your good offices. Can we talk again on Wednesday about what we have and go from there. I think our next steps will be to talk to these guys and see what they can tell us. Call you Wednesday at 10:30? I want to give you some time to get to the office!"

"You can play me!" said Terry. "I am up and running here at 07:30 along with Tommy."

"Boy, does that sound familiar." said Sean," First to practice and last to leave."

They wrapped up the call with some more small talk and Brad went off to a mediation appointment. Sean went back to his office at the school and looked over the Fall schedule. Damn, Elmira High for the first game. Always tough whenever you played them. The home of the "Elmira Express", Ernie Davis who went on to play at Syracuse. So talented and gone so soon. Tommy, we need you back on the team. It's going to be a challenge this year.

Then his mind went back to the Bonneville. Where were they? They had some leads but no knock-out punch at this point. Maybe that was how these things worked. Small steps and eventually you got there. The lead he liked best was the name from the 1985 VIN. But that was over 35 years ago. Was the guy even alive now? Would he remember anything? How old would he be? Late 70s or 80s and would he be firing on all cylinders at this point?

As agreed, they called Terry in Harrisburg on Wednesday morning. She was ready to go, all business.

"How're we looking?" asked Brad.

Terry filled them in on the progress to date, which essentially eliminated any blanket search of DMV records. But she was able to find addresses for the VIN number from 1985 and 1996

"Here's the thing with Mr. 1985," Terry said. The guy died two years ago. But his wife is still alive, and he has a son who is alive. Both are in the Scranton area. Mr. 1996 is alive and around. He lives south of Scranton in a town called Freeland, near Hazelton."

"We'll talk to both of them." said Brad. "Sean can call ahead to make sure they are okay with meeting us."

"Will do," said Sean, "and we can stop by Carl's place in Clarks Summit and return his club stuff. Also, I have the library magazines to return."

"Sounds like you have a full day," Terry said.

"By the way, Terry, have you kept Tommy up to speed on your activity? I don't want the head prosecutor on my back!" asked Brad.

"I sure have; he's copied on a daily basis," replied Terry," and no pushback from his office. In fact, there are some folks here who remember the history of the case and have been following your adventures."

"I hope we don't disappoint them." said Sean. He seemed discouraged with the lack of progress.

"It's always like that," said Brad, sensing his disappointment. "Then a door opens up. You never know where the door is or when it will be opened but it does happen. The trick now is to not get discouraged."

"Okay, Terry," said Brad. "If Sean can get us lined up, we'll make a loop through PA next week. "Once we get that under our belt, we should have a better feel for what our next steps will be."

"I'll continue looking into the DMV records," said Terry. "Maybe I can get lucky and find some other stuff."

"Maybe find the holy grail?" said Sean.

"I think Indiana Jones has already done that!"

After they finished the call with Terry, Sean and Brad reviewed the material again and Brad tried to reassure the coach they were making progress, even though it might not seem like it. He thought there might be issues here not understood or not spoken. Brad was worried Sean had such an emotional investment in the case that if they were not successful, it would be devastating for him. To date, they had not uncovered a lot of information, just bits and pieces but nothing solid. Maybe that was all there was. End of story. But why was this so important to Sean. Had he known Eddie other than as a neighborhood kid? At the time, Sean was twelve and Eddie eight so there was probably not a social connection between them. So why was Eddie so important? Was Sean telling him everything?

Brad decided he had to ask the hard question.

"Sean, help me out." said Brad, "Before we head to PA next week, tell me why Eddie is so important to you. I know the crime was horrific and I'm not trying to diminish it, but I know there is more to this as far as you're concerned. You need to let me know so we are both on the same page. Were you close to Eddie? Was he close to someone in your family? Maybe your younger brother Dan? What?"

"I'm sorry Brad," said Sean, "I wasn't trying to hold any information from you. Eddie and Danny were good neighborhood friends. They were pretty close in age. I used to see a lot of Eddie around the neighborhood and at our house. But, candidly, he was one of the younger guys and we did not hang out together."

"Okay I get that. Then what is driving you so hard now?"

"It's my dad," said Sean, "when he was dying, he was able to be at home and I spent a lot of time with him. We really got to know each other then. Not just father and son but two guys talking about stuff. We got very close. I cried in front of him and he in front of me. We had no more barriers at that point. Don't forget, we're Irish and that's not in the playbook."

He thought for a moment and then went on. "I think as you get older you tend to relive all your past life events, the good ones and the ones that definitely wish you could redo. A major regret in my dad's life was not being able to find Eddie. He and Eddie had bonded. Eddie always looked for Pop when he came over to our house. For some reason, the two of them got along like a father and son. When Eddie was abducted, Pop was devastated. He spent the reminder of his career and retirement years trying to find him. He never could close out the case and it stayed with him till the end. Before Pop lapsed into a coma and died, we were talking about Eddie. I don't remember how it came up but there it was. I told Pop I would keep looking for Eddie. At that point I had no idea what to do or how to do it. Mom and I were there, each holding a hand. He looked over at me and I squeezed his hand and said I'd keep looking. He squeezed my hand too, then he looked over at mom, said I love you and just faded away. That was around eight years ago. Then the picture of the car came out in the Times-Tribune and it was as if Pop had reached back to me and said, Sean, time to get to work."

"Thanks," said Brad, "That's not easy stuff to talk about. Look we'll do the best we can and whatever falls out we'll live with it. The fact that you're here and invested in this process would make your Dad proud."

Chapter 9

A FAMILIAR DRIVE BACK to Scranton. They both had been doing it for years. As they were driving past Great Bend, PA, just over the NY state line, Brad started to look around at the terrain off the highway.

"You remember the big floods we had in the area about ten years ago?"

"Sure do." said Sean. "We had water in our basement and my brother in law had big problems. He lives over by MacArthur school and got hit pretty bad."

"Well, I was driving by this area shortly after the flood back then and Great Bend was no more, it was No Bend. The river completely overflowed the banks and went in a straight line through the town. It was amazing to see. I always try to reimagine it every time I come by here."

They had the contact list from Terry. Sean had called the people to set up meeting times. They would drop off the magazines in between. Mr. 1985 was first as he had the best potential. Actually, Mr. 1985 was dead, but Terry had found a son. The sequence would be son of Mr. 1985, then the Holmes library. After that Mr. 1996 and a stop by Carl's in Clark Summit on the way home.

Mr. 1985 was named Charles Burrell. His son apparently went by Chuck.

He smiled and said, "Charles for dad, Chuck for me. Don't ask me why, but that's how it was growing up. My mom is with me today, visiting from her nursing home. Her name is Doreen and she's in the living room. I thought maybe she might be able to help in your search."

"Thanks Chuck." said Brad. "Why don't we meet your mom and we can ask you both our questions. Save you the trouble of going over plowed ground twice."

"Sounds good," said Chuck, leading them into the living room where an elderly lady was sitting in a chair, a blanket over her knees. "Mom, here are the gentlemen from Binghamton who are searching for information on one of the cars Dad used to own."

Sean guessed that Doreen was in her late eighties. She was very alert and was eager to talk about the old days.

Brad started out. "Mrs. Burrell, Doreen, thank you for agreeing to talk with us. We're investigating the ownership of a 1975 blue Pontiac Bonneville, trying to get a complete list of who owned it over the years. We understand your late husband had it for a while. If you don't mind answering a few questions, we're hoping it will help us develop a trail back to the original owner."

"Why do you care so much about this car?" asked the old lady.

Sean said," we think it may have been the car used in an abduction of a young boy back in 1975,"

"1975?" said Doreen. She thought for a moment. "I do remember something about a kidnapping or disappearance of a child back then."

"It was an abduction," said Sean. "I was 12 at the time and lived on Spring Street in Scranton. I actually saw it happen. I was sitting on my front steps and saw Eddie Filmore get into the car. I never forgot its make or color. Recently, I saw a picture of what I'm sure is the same car in the Times-Tribune. It won an award at a local antique car show. I am hoping that if we find the original owner, we can find out what happened to Eddie."

Brad asked, "do you have any paperwork about the car from back then?"

"I don't think so," said Chuck. "Usually the paperwork about the car goes with it when it is sold. The antique car guys are anal about that stuff.

Also a few years after dad died, we did a big cleanout of the garage and shop, so anything about the car is probably long gone."

"But Chuckie," Doreen said, "I do remember the car some. Charles bought it as an antique car investment. It was only 10 years old at the time and was not yet qualified as an antique. He planned to hold on to it. He said in time he would have a real good antique. I remember the car had hardly any miles on it. That car was to be our big retirement trip someday."

"How long did you keep it?" asked Sean.

"Maybe 8-10 years" said Doreen "But it never really moved up in value as we thought it would. I guess it was just another nice sedan. Charles said we needed a more special type of car to get a good increase in price."

Chuck added, "I guess that's why dad started looking at Corvettes and Thunderbirds."

"I think so," said Doreen. "We did well on a couple of them. Dad liked them because they were production cars and you could find them around here."

Now for the hard question, thought Sean. Who owned it before Charles? Had it been through yet another owner?

"Do you know who he bought the car from?" asked Brad.

"Sorry I don't. At least not by name," replied Doreen, "Charles worked for RCA here in those days and I'm pretty sure it was a guy at work who needed some money. I remember him saying that the guy had it only a year or so."

"Yeah, I remember him saying something along that line." Chuck agreed. "I was in my teens then and would hang around the shop with dad."

"Do you know who the RCA guy bought the car from?" asked Brad.

"No I don't" said Doreen but I think it had to be local. I remember Charles said his friend told him it was in storage up on blocks, all covered up. Maybe that guy was thinking the same thing. Keep it in good shape and make some money off it. It had to have been in storage as there were hardly any miles on it."

"Mom's right," said Chuck. "I think the guy from dad's work bought it from storage and wanted to do the same thing. Keep it and wait for the value to go up. Dad certainly had the same game plan. Dad told me it had under 3,000 miles on it."

Brad thought about what he had just heard. The car was owned for eight plus years by Charles Burrell. He bought the car from a work friend who had stored it. The work friend had bought it from a local guy who had also kept it in storage. Maybe a little better timeline now. 1975 to 1984 with the original owner, then on to the RCA guy for a year and then on to Charles Burrell. No names for the RCA guy or the original owner. Chuck said the car had under 3,000 miles on it so it made sense it must have been in storage most of its earlier life. That explained the lack of records. Time to move on to Mr. 2010, thought Brad.

They stopped off at the Holmes library to return the magazines. The same librarian was on duty and she was happy to see Sean.

"Hello to my main researcher," she said, "any luck?"

"Yeah, a bit thanks. But we didn't break the code yet. This is my friend Brad who is helping me out with my work."

"Nice to meet you ma'am, thanks for taking such good care of Sean. The magazines were really useful."

The drive south to Freeland was a bit under an hour. They stopped at a Subway for some lunch on the way down. Sean had a gift card from his kids, his Father's Day present. When they got to Mr. 2010 whose name was Ted Davis, they found him on the front porch. It almost seemed like he was waiting for them. He was a tall, slim man who had aged well. Good genes and lifestyle. Sean thought, note to self, stay with the exercise program dummy! Moira's right!

"Thanks for meeting with us Mr. Davis," Sean said. "This is my colleague Brad Petronella who is helping me with the search."

Sean went through the background on the search as he had done with Doreen and Chuck Burrell earlier. They'd been happy to help. The same held for Ted Davis.

When Sean finished Ted said, "I don't really remember this kid Eddie Filmore, sorry to say, but if I can provide any information to help you, I am happy to do so."

"Great," said Brad, "let me ask you some questions and see where we can take this. First of all, how long did you own the car?"

"About 5 to 6 years, I took it to shows around the northeast. Mostly local stuff that I drove the car to, but for the out of state shows, I trailered the car to them."

"What about documentation when you bought the car?" asked Brad.

"The guy had a shoe box full of papers on it. Bills from servicing and small repairs, old DMV stuff and car show awards. I knew him from previous shows, so I was comfortable with the purchase. It had very few miles on it and that was the main attraction. And as always rust. The old cars didn't have the material and treatments to fight rust and that was always a problem. Once you start patching rust areas, the value goes down a lot. A clean car is key."

"Do you remember seeing the car at antique shows over the years before you bought it?" asked Sean.

"Not way back, but that does not surprise me. It would not have been old enough to qualify as an antique until around 2000, so 1975 to 2000 was a bit like ageing a bottle of wine. If you want to offer something in the original condition, you have no choice but to park it and let it age. When I bought the car in 2010, its ticket was punched, it was an antique."

"Why did you sell it?" asked Sean.

"The usual reasons," answered Ted, "to move on up the value ladder and frankly, you sort of get bored with the same car after a while. Maybe like looking for a new girlfriend. Surprisingly, most of the car sales are between collectors. Like I said, I bought the car from a guy at a local show. Wrote him a check and that was it. A lot of cars are bought and sold like this."

Brad had always felt that Mr. 2010 was too far removed from 1975 to be of any direct help but you never discount a source. You have to run them all to ground. They thanked Ted for his time and decided to head back to Binghamton, with a stop along the way to give Carl back his stuff. Sean did not talk much on the way to Clarks Summit. Brad could sense his frustration; he probably felt they might be at the end of the line.

"Look Sean," he said, "let's not jump off the cliff just yet. We'll go back to Binghamton and go over all we have and see if we can find another angle or approach. We have good support from Harrisburg, maybe Terry can give us a steer. Sales tax records, whatever."

"Yeah, you're right," answered Sean. "You've been great with your time and help. I couldn't have taken this up to this point without your participation. Come what may, I feel I've met my promise to Pop. I tried, I really tried."

When they got to Clarks Summit, Carl was in his garage puttering around. Sean introduced Brad.

"Thinking of getting another car?" said Brad.

"Oh no!" My wife would kill me and bury me in it!"

"She is always tidying up and another car is the last thing she wants around here. Speaking of which, I've a shoe box of old papers for the Bonneville. I forgot about it when you were here before. I didn't want to keep the box in the garage as the heat, cold and humidity would destroy the papers over a few years. So, I parked it all in the closet in the hall and forgot about it. My wife found it the other day and was asking what I wanted to do with it. Sorry, Sean, I never thought about it when we were together earlier."

When Brad heard the word *shoe box*, he could feel the hairs stand up on the back of his neck. *Shoe box*! The same words Ted Davis had used. Maybe this was a path back to the original owner? Or probably it was just another dead end. He hoped Sean wouldn't get all fired up again.

Hopefully, he just viewed the box as some more paperwork to be sifted. They thanked Carl for his time, took the box and got back into the car.

Brad told Sean he would keep the box with him and look at it over the weekend. He tried to downplay it. "Probably just a record of oil changes," he said.

Sean was subdued and just nodded.

They agreed to meet at the Resolution Center on Monday and call Terry to keep her up to speed. Brad was happy to be working with Terry. She was a good kid who saw the opportunities and not the problems. Why does that seem to change as we get older? Maybe working with Terry would reverse the process? Anyway, it was Friday night. Scotch night. Clearly a two-scotch problem!

At home, with a Scotch in front of him, Brad carefully started to review the shoe box material. It was clear that the paperwork was earlier than what they had seen so far. In 1977 and 1978 there was some local work done on the car. Nothing dramatic. Tire leak repair, oil change, new coolant fluid, etc. Just the stuff you do regardless of the use of the car. What made all this interesting was that on some of the bills was an address. A small town just outside Carbondale called Mayfield. Maybe a small farm? Let's find out thought Brad.

He immediately called Sean and told him what he had discovered.

"We caught a break Sean. Some of this paper may go back to the original owner. I found stuff from 1977/1978 with an address!"

"Then we got it! cried Sean.

"Not so fast," said Brad. "We've got an address. Another place to look. That's all. We need Terry to chase down the name and see who is still there and whatever else she can discover. This is our best shot. We need to thoroughly assess it."

Sean met with Brad at the Resolution Center on Monday and they called Terry.

"Terry, this is your favorite investigative team calling," said Brad.

"I missed you guys." said Terry, "How did you make out this weekend?"

"I think we got lucky," said Brad. "I've got a name and address that gets very close to 1975. I'm texting it over. Can you check it out and see if anyone is still there and also take a look at the census and tax records to see who else may have lived there?"

Terry said, "I'll need a few days to look at birth and death certificates. Please don't tell me the name is Smith or Jones!"

"Ha, you funny guy," said Brad, "the name is Chetsky and first name is Phil. Sounds like a contraction of a much longer Eastern European name. A lot of times folks did that getting off the boat or the immigration clerks did it for them."

"We'll be okay if the name was changed way back. We need a few generations not something done last month," said Terry

"Well, it was Chetsky in 1975 for sure," replied Brad.

"Let's talk Wednesday afternoon," said Terry "that will give me the better part of two days to chase this down. We are only working with one name; I should be able to get there."

Sean stopped by his office at the school on the way home to check on the Fall schedule. Junior was there looking over some player profiles and upcoming games.

"How is your AAU team looking?" asked Sean "You booked hotel rooms for the championship round yet?"

"Maybe in a week or so," said Junior. "Can I ask you a question?"

"Sure."

"You know Spud's kid Jaime?" asked Junior. "I like the kid and he has a game to play. I'm just worried about moving him along too quickly. The thing is he does not understand how good he is and how good he can be. I don't want to put him where he is not comfortable and hurt his development,"

"Makes sense. How many guys do you have on the team?"

Junior replied, "We have ten guys and may pick up another. But let's count on 10."

"Good, and you told me you would be playing all your guys in every game."

"Sure," said Junior, "I don't want any kid playing AAU ball and just sit on the bench."

"Well," said Sean, "I think as he plays, Jaime will show you where he is in the development cycle. You can adjust his playing time to get a good fit and not have him trying to play over his head. Basketball is a great game for rotating guys in and out of the lineup. Also, talk this over with the senior lad you called out during your opening meeting, Rahim?"

"Yeah, he's a senior and will be our floor leader. The kids like him a lot."

"Talk to him," said Sean, "let him know what you are thinking and have the same conversation about the other seniors too. Make them part of the team development."

"You got it Coach, thanks," said Junior. "You make it sound so logical and easy."

"Just curious, where is Rahim going after graduation?"

"He has some great offers from around the state." said Junior "he wants to stay in NY and has not looked much outside of the state. Syracuse, Buffalo, Colgate, Union and Hamilton. Maybe Williams over in MA also."

"Great schools," said Sean "I wish him the best."

"He'll do fine, He has a strong support network at home and the family will do the right thing. Personally, I don't think Rahim is a true NBA impact player. If he plays Division 1 ball in college, he will probably be drafted, but it's hard. You get drafted and then have 2 years to find a home. After that it can be a long wind down through International ball clubs, and once there you tend to bounce from contract to contract. My advice is to go for the education and don't let the sport define your future. But I'm comfortable his family will make sure he ends up in the right place."

Chapter 10

WHEN HE GOT HOME, SEAN reviewed the latest developments in the Bonneville search with Moira. She was always a great sounding board. Always ready to listen first and then comment. It was nice to go over it with her and get her perspective. Like Brad she cautioned Sean to not wear his heart on his sleeve. This was going to work, or it wasn't.

"The outcome will not define you Sean." she said. "You loved your dad and were a good son. You've done your very best to continue his work on the case. But if it doesn't close, it does not diminish you as a person. You're still my Coach!"

On Wednesday afternoon, Brad and Sean called Terry in Harrisburg.

"How're we doing Terry? Any joy?"

"Yeah I think so, I was able to cross check some of the records so I am pretty comfortable with what I've found. After flailing with the DMV records, this was more straightforward. Looks like the Chetsky name has been with the family since Grandpa got off the boat. I don't really know if it is a contraction but does not matter as all our records are for Chetsky."

"How many are we dealing with?" asked Brad.

"Not that many. I was able to find the family on census records in Mayfield before the turn of the century. Then mom, dad, Phil and another brother, Stanley, from a later census. I think it's this family of four we're concerned with. Mom and dad are dead. Phil still lives in Mayfield and Stanley lives in Scranton. Stanly is the oldest, born in 1952 and brother Phil in 1955."

"Great!" said Brad, we need to get back to Scranton this weekend and talk to these guys."

"Should I call ahead?" asked Sean. "Terry has contact numbers."

"No," Brad answered, after thinking a moment. "Let's not call ahead. We're getting close to these guys and I don't want to give anyone a chance to think about us or concoct a story. Let's just show up with our smiling faces and sparkling personalities."

They decided to talk to the older brother first. So early on Saturday morning, it was down I- 81S again. They arrived at Stanley's address in Scranton around 09:30AM and decided to just drive by and see what was going on at the house. There were two cars in the driveway, so there could be a Mrs. Chetsky or grown kids. They parked away from the house and waited. About 10:00 AM an older woman came out and got into a Ford Focus and drove off. Based on her apparent age, they thought she must be his wife.

"Okay Sean, let's ring the bell."

When the door opened, Brad introduced himself and Sean. "Mr. Chetsky I am conducting an investigation with support from the Attorney General in Harrisburg. I would like to take a few minutes and ask you some questions about a 1975 Pontiac Bonneville four-door hardtop."

"My old Pontiac?" said Stanley. "Whatever for? I sold that car ages ago, must be 30 or 35 years now. What interest could anyone have in that old car? Surely Mr. Petronella, you must have more important things to look into."

"I'm most interested in a date in 1975. August specifically, Mr. Chetsky."

Did Chetsky flinch or tighten some face muscles wondered Brad. It was nothing dramatic but there was something. Brad did not say anything, he wanted to keep the conversation going. Sean might have picked up on the tension but he did not say anything.

After a brief period of silence, Stanley spoke. 'Well, as I remember in 1975 through all of July and August, I was in the VA hospital in Wilkes Barre. I had a ruptured appendix but didn't know it. I drove back to

Scranton after being discharged from the Army at Ft. Hood, TX. By the time I got home, I was in bad shape and ended up at the VA hospital in Wilkes Barre. They were not sure when my appendix ruptured so they admitted me even though I wasn't active Army anymore. My intestines were a mess and I had lost a lot of blood from internal bleeding. They estimated I had gone 2-4 days in that state. I shouldn't have survived, according to the doctors."

"Was the drive to Scranton with the Pontiac?"

"Yeah, I bought it at Ft Hood from a local dealer. He gave great military discounts. Only paid around $4,400 as I remember. We'll never see those prices again." He looked thoughtful for a minute, as if seeing his younger self. "Put a temporary TX paper plate on it and headed north along with the best golf clubs I could buy at the PX: MacGregors! While I was in the hospital, the car was in Mayfield. My brother Phil looked after it. I was an Electronics Officer in Army communications. While I was recuperating at the VA, I landed a job with a company that serviced communication equipment at US Embassies. I worked for them the next 26 years or so. Travelled and lived all over the world. The car ended up in storage in the barn in Mayfield. I was not around and not sure about what I wanted to do with it. Keep it or sell it. Finally in 1985 or so I sold it.

"Does Phil have a driver's license"?

"Yes, but he doesn't drive anymore. You have to understand that Phil is a very simple person. His IQ is very low. Border line, if you know what I mean. He managed to get a license and that was the high point of his life, He loved that license."

"Mr. Chetsky, I think your car and maybe your brother may have been involved in the abduction of a child in August of 1975. A kid by the name of Eddie Filmore."

"No, no, no!" exclaimed Stanley. "That's just not possible. Phil is a simple guy and has lived a very quiet life over the years. He is not a child molester or some kind of predator. That's not my brother. Go away and leave us alone. Phil's done nothing wrong. I'm not going to talk to you anymore."

Sean was clearly disturbed by the conversation but kept his silence. Brad had not been abrasive but knew where this was headed. He needed to keep Stanley on board.

Stanley continued, "Anyway how do you know it was my car? There are lots of Pontiacs around, still are, even though they don't make them anymore. Maybe it was stolen. Did someone see him in the car?

"Mr. Chetsky," said Brad, "We really don't know for sure if your brother was involved. But we do know that a 1975 Pontiac Bonneville identical to your car was involved in Eddie's abduction and the car was never found. It just disappeared. Now I have to report back to the Attorney General what I have uncovered. I expect they will have the local law enforcement or state police follow up. Once this happens it's out of my hands. Based on what you have told us about Phil, I think a better way forward is if we, that is Sean, you and I talk to Phil before the legal system gets turned on. Let's listen to his explanation. He could be entirely innocent."

"Oh God Phil, what have you done?" said Stanley, all the fight going out of him suddenly. "Please tell me you were not part of anything like this." Turning to Brad, he said, "Please don't tell me he was involved in this, not my brother Phil."

"Mr. Chetsky, we just don't know," said Brad. "I think you should call him, and we'll go meet with him."

Mayfield is north of Scranton, south of Carbondale, so not a long a drive. Stanley called Phil to make sure he would be around and the three headed over to the old family farm. Brad and Sean did not talk much during the drive. Each was lost in his own thoughts. Stanley tried to calm his fears by talking. He told them how his brother had always been slow and had stayed at home with his mother. He told them that Phil worked in a sheltered workshop in Scranton. A van would pick him up in the morning and drop him off in the afternoon. He had learned basic housekeeping skills and was proud of the house and its appearance.

After their mother died, a deacon from Phil's church looked after the financial side until Stanley returned to Scranton. Stanley took over managing the daily financial running of the house. Utilities, taxes, repairs were on his side of the ledger. Some tasks Phil could do, but when needed, Stanley was there. Phil led a very simple life, happy in his orbit of church and job. He did not go out much at all. Stanley said his brother was not good with strangers and got easily alarmed. Brad wondered if he knew more that he was telling them but did not push it with him.

When they got there, they could see what Stanley meant. The house was lost in a time warp. It was clean and well maintained but the colors and furnishings were from another time. It reminded Sean of his house on Spring street when he was growing up. They talked about how to start asking Phil about the date and car. They agreed that it would be best if Stanley started the conversation and asked the initial questions.

Phil was waiting for them, clearly not aware or concerned about a potential problem or issue. He introduced Brad and Sean as investigators trying to sort out a missing car.

Stanley started out, "Phil do remember our 1975 Pontiac Bonneville that was in the barn some years back?"

"You know I do," said Phil, "it was a sweet car and you had me take care of it for you while you were in the hospital back then. I did a real good job."

"You did Phil," said Stanley "and I always knew you would do a good job."

"Phil, did you ever drive the car?" asked Stanley. "I know you had a driver's license."

Phil did not want to answer and would not make eye contact with his brother. Stanley asked again. Phil still did not answer and was becoming agitated.

"I won't get mad at you Phil," said Stanley "but I need to know. It's very important."

Finally, Phil said, "yes, when you were in the hospital. The car was so new and shiny and smelled so nice with all the leather. Just a couple of times. I had my new license so I could drive it."

"Where did you go Phil?" asked Stanley. "A big trip or just around the town?"

"Once around the yard and the field road to make sure I knew how to do it, and then once in town." said Phil.

"Around town, that's pretty good." said Stanley. "Mayfield?"

"No man, Scranton. It was cool. I had the radio on and all the windows down!"

"Wow, I wish I'd been there." said Stanley. "Did you meet anybody?"

At that point Phil got very nervous. He seemed to be grappling with long suppressed memories. He started rocking backwards and forwards. Brad recognized this as a coping mechanism used by people in the grips of extreme emotion. Stanley seemed at a loss as to how to take this forward. Brad was afraid he would refuse to continue and risk upsetting his brother more. He spoke up for the first time.

"Phil," he said gently, "sometimes things are very hard to think about and even harder to talk about. But Stanley is here and he loves you very much. It's important for all of us to understand what happened that day and you are the only one who can tell us. Please help us."

Phil did not say anything for a few minutes. It was clear he was trying to process the rush of emotion and information. He probably did not understand himself what happened and he'd kept it suppressed for many years. Now it was all in front of him and begging to be released.

"It wasn't my fault. He wouldn't stop crying," he said at last.

"What wasn't your fault?" asked Brad.

"I got lost and really scared. I had to get the car back and Eddie got scared too, started crying and wanted to get out of the car. I pulled over and told Eddie to stop but he wouldn't. He tried to jump out but I pulled him back and shook him to get him to stop crying. He kept crying and I shook him harder. Then he just stopped and would not wake up."

Stanley was quietly sobbing at this point and Sean felt as if he had been hit by a freight train. Stanley and Sean had no experience of this type of thing. It was all happening so fast. Too hard to comprehend at this point. Brad needed to know how to connect Phil and Eddie. Why did Eddie get in the car? Did he know Phil? Why would the boy get into a stranger's car?

"Phil, did you know Eddie?" asked Brad.

"Sort of," said Phil. "His church group of kids used to meet with our church group to play games and talk. Eddie was a nice kid, I liked him."

"How did you find him?"

"I was driving down a street and saw him. I pulled over and asked him if he wanted to go for a ride in my big brother's car. I showed him my driver's license so he would know I was safe. He said okay and got in."

"Where did you go?"

"I don't know, around town," said Phil.

"Then you got lost?"

"Yeah, Eddie wanted to go down some streets to see if a friend of his was around to show him the car. But he wasn't and I needed to get the car back or Stanley would be mad. I was lost and Eddie was too. He started crying and yelling he wanted to go home. He kept grabbing the steering wheel. It was dangerous! I stopped the car and told him to keep quiet, but he just kept crying and shouting. He tried to get out, but it was a bad neighborhood and I didn't want him to be on the streets. I shook him and shook him and suddenly he went quiet. He went to sleep."

"How did you find your way out?"

"I don't know. I sort of found a place I knew after driving around."

"Was Eddie still asleep?"

"Yeah, I tried over and over to wake him but he wouldn't move, I think he went to heaven." Tears were running down Phil's face.

"What did you do then?" Brad's voice was very even and gentle.

"I drove by my house and then out into the country nearby where the woods are. I carried him into the trees and put him down on the leaves for when he woke up. I came back there the next day. He was still there, and he was very cold, so I knew he went to heaven. I found a safe place for him and put him in there. I made it nice and deep so he would be safe. I used to go up there on hikes and talk to him. Tell him I was sorry."

By now, Stanley was distraught, quietly crying and trying to process what had happened. Sean put his arm around the man's shoulders to try and offer some comfort. It was a tragic sequence of events. No one felt better knowing the truth. Eddie hadn't been the target of a predator. Phil had been forced to re-live the agony of something he knew he'd done wrong and had tried to fix. Stanley blamed himself for leaving that tempting car there to be driven. The closure Sean thought he'd get was replaced by a great sense of sadness, both for Eddie and for Phil, who had been marked forever. Brad usually felt good when the truth finally emerged, but this time, he felt hollow. All they had done was unwrap a crime that the justice system wouldn't be able to effectively deal with. Brad thought about what to do with the information.

After some time, he spoke. "Stanley, you are going to have to trust me now," he said. "I need to talk to a someone I know and trust at the AGs office in Harrisburg about the next steps. Are you okay with this?"

"I really don't know you guys, but I don't think you came down here to arrest a murderer." said Stanley. "I'll go with you on this."

"Okay, take care of Phil and I'll be back to you early next week."

After that Sean and Brad left for Binghamton. Stanley spent the night with Phil to try to help him get back his equilibrium. Having to re-live the awful events he'd submerged for so long had shaken him almost speechless. On the way home, Sean tried to come to grips with all that had happened. Had they caught a killer? Not really. Had they solved a crime? He guessed so, but what crime? What were they going to do now? He didn't know.

At home he went through the day's events with Moira. She listened to the whole story before commenting.

"I'm at a loss for words, Sean. I can't imagine going through all of that in one day."

"I'm worried about Phil now. Putting him in jail would probably kill him. He would not be able to comprehend what is happening. I don't think he really understands what he did to Eddie. He was only a teenager back then and his mental acuity has always been severely limited. Its broken Stanley's heart today when this all came out. What have we done? Two lives changed forever. Now they both have to live with this. On top of it all, Eddie's death was senseless. The poor kid got into a car. The driver panicked and then Eddie did too. Then he ended up dead. God, what have I done? What have I done? I wrecked two lives and for what? Justice? There is no justice in this."

Moira replied, "Sean, you were not the cause of this and certainly not the person who has to carry the load in the future. I don't know what the next steps are going to be, but I know Tommy will look into this and do the best he can for Phil and Stanley. You have to trust him. Brad too."

Monday morning, Brad and Sean called Tommy and Terry and told them the story. Not a lot was said until after he finished. Then, in a measured tone, Tommy went over it all again, in detail, taking notes. He focused on Stanley and Phil. How it all fit together, the ruptured appendix, the jobs overseas, the car stored for years so it had very low mileage, its apparent disappearance, the young boy with special needs eager to show his friend the cool car he was driving. After that the line was quiet for a few minutes.

"I don't see where sending Phil to jail will serve any purpose," said Tommy "but we have to address the issue of Eddie's death. Phil will have to serve some sort of sentence, but it's best in a psychiatric hospital. He will need treatment and help in understanding what he did. There's a state hospital in Clarks Summit. I don't know a lot about it but it could be a good place for him. If not, then the state hospital in Norristown is a good choice. I would prefer Clarks Summit so that Stanley can easily visit him."

"What happens after that?" asked Sean.

"I don't know," said Tommy. "He may be released to a half-way house or possibly released into care with Stanley. He isn't a danger to society. But even if all of this had not happened, I don't see him living independently for much longer. We'll have to see how the treatment goes and what the Docs think about the future for him. I have to check with the boss on this before we take the next steps. This was a murder after all, and we need to make sure we're on solid ground. I'll get back to you as quickly as I can."

"Okay." Brad agreed. "And I also think Stanley should seek therapy, He was not aware of any of this until Friday. It's been a terrible shock to him."

"I agree" said Tommy, "but we need to sort out Phil first."

Tommy called the next day to confirm that the Attorney General agreed with the course of action. They set up a meeting with Stanley on Wednesday. He was the center of Phil's life now. On Wednesday, Brad, Sean, a State Police investigator and Dr. Malkovich, a psychiatrist from the state hospital at Clarks Summit met at Stanley's house to discuss the next steps. They decided it was best for Stanley to explain to his brother that he had to go to the hospital for a little while to get better and help him understand what really had happened.

Stanley started the conversation quietly saying to Phil, "I know you've been worried all these years about what happened to Eddie. You would not drive again and you kept visiting him where he's sleeping. You kept it all inside your head and it's not good for you. We need to help you get better and not have to worry about it all the time. There's a hospital in Clarks Summit where they can help you and I can visit you while you're there."

"How long will I be there?" Phil asked him.

"It's hard to say, but I promise we'll make you better," answered the psychiatrist.

"And Stanley can come and see me?"

"Anytime," Doctor Malkovich said, "he'll be helping us also."

It went a lot smoother than they had expected. Phil had been carrying Eddie's death in his subconscious for a long time, even when he didn't know he was thinking about it. It had made him constantly nervous, unable to focus. He was ready to get well. After Stanley, Doctor Malkovich and the state police investigator left with Phil to go to Clarks Summit, Brad and Sean sat in the front yard at Phil's house and talked.

Chapter 11

"YOU KNOW BRAD," HE said, "it's not finished yet."

"I figured as much. Who's left from Eddie's family?"

"Two brothers and their mother who's in a nursing home. I remember them and I'm sure they remember me. It was a tight neighborhood."

Sean had their phone numbers and they decided to speak with the brothers first. They weren't sure about the health of Eddie's mother. The brothers, Dan and Mike still lived in the area. Sean called the older brother Dan, reintroduced himself and asked if he could stop by. Dan assumed it was a social call but when Sean asked if Mike could also be there, he knew it was something more.

"What's up?" he asked suspiciously.

"I have some news about Eddie."

"Oh my God." said Dan. "After all these years. What's going on?"

"Let's talk about it in person," said Sean. "It's complicated."

They met up at Dan's house in the early afternoon. Mike was already there and had an anxious look about him.

"I always knew something like this would happen," said Mike. "Someday, some way this would all come back. Eddie is dead? Right?"

"Yes Mike," said Sean, "I'll tell you all about it. It will take some time."

Sean told him about seeing the picture in the newspaper and how he had gotten Brad's help with the investigation. Brad explained how they had searched and what the outcome was. When he finished the brothers were silent. Mike was stifling sobs and Dan had teared up. Brad and Sean excused themselves and went into the front yard to allow the brothers to talk between themselves. After thirty minutes or so Dan came to the door and asked them back into the house.

"My first thought was to get the guy's name and kill him," said Dan, "but it doesn't solve any problems and will only hurt us all more. I still have thoughts of revenge of some sort. I need to deal with it and I will. The whole thing is so stupid and senseless, I can't believe it happened."

"It's senseless and impossible to comprehend," said Brad, "people get killed crossing the street or shot because they are in the wrong place. Such a waste of life."

"Do we really know it's Eddie?" asked Mike. "It's been a long time."

"The state forensics team is at the site now and are recovering the remains. They'll get some DNA samples from the both of you to confirm a match."

Mike said, "Eddie broke his left arm and they had to put a pin in the bone. Maybe they can see that."

"I'll pass it on."

"What do we tell Mom?" said Dan. "She's doing okay for her age but she's fragile. I don't know if she can handle it all. Maybe we should just let it be?"

Brad said, "Dan as much as this has been on your mind over the years, it's been worse for your mother. Moms always worry about their children. When they disappear and don't know what happened to them, it's terrible. You should try and tell her; you can find a way. All of you need closure."

"You're right," said Dan. "I just need to sort out how to do it."

"You don't have to do it today," said Brad. "Give it some time."

On the way back, there was not much conversation between Sean and Brad. Sean was completely spent and alone with his thoughts. Brad was organizing the report he'd have to send to Tommy in Harrisburg. It needed to be comprehensive.

"Rest well Pop, we found Eddie."

At last Sean had closure.

Just a young lad off on a car ride on a lazy Summer afternoon.

Epilogue

ABOUT A MONTH LATER, Sean called and told Brad he had received a funeral notice from Dan Filmore. There was to be a funeral mass and burial for Eddie at St. Paul's in Scranton the coming Saturday. They were invited to the 10AM service. On Saturday they drove down to Scranton.

The church was not crowded. Eddie had died so young he had not developed a defined group of friends and many who knew him or the family had died or moved out of the neighborhood. But there were familiar faces from the old neighborhood and the surrounding area who remembered Eddie, Sean and their families. They smiled and nodded as Sean and Brad came into the church. Dan and Mike were there with their mother. Father Gene asked everyone to move up to the front pews as the gathering was small and he wanted them to be close, like a family.

Dan delivered a touching eulogy about his youngest brother and how as the baby of the family he was the spark plug. He reminded everyone of the time Eddie put corn flakes in his older brother's socks and what it was like finding that out on a cold winter's morning trying to get ready for school.

Mike told about reading stories to Eddie and how he would try to change the narrative of the story. Eddie would make him do it over until it matched the story in the book.

Sean spoke about the energetic kid who would come over to their house and wait for his father to come home from work. His dad and Eddie had a close relationship. When Eddie went missing he told of his search for him over many years.

The internment at the cemetery was brief, Father Gene blessed the ground, the casket and the mourners. Eddie's mom stood briefly and put some flowers on her son's grave. During the ceremony, Sean nudged Brad and glanced at a slight hill about 60 yards away. Standing by a tree was Stanley Chetsky.

After the burial they met at Dan's house for coffee and a buffet lunch. Brad and Sean met Eddie's mother.

"I do remember you Sean," she said, "and your family. You father was so good to me during the troubles and never forget about Eddie. And you never did either, Sean, just like your father. He would be proud of you. I do hope the other boy will find some peace! Such a waste, two lives lost actually."

Then she turned to Brad. "And Mr. Petronella, thank you for helping my boys to tell me about Eddie. I don't have much time left these days but now I know where my Eddie is at last. God bless you."

hil was released from the psychiatric hospital in Clarks Summit after 18 months. Stanley visited him regularly while he was there and was helpful in his treatment. Phil was released to Stanley's care and moved into his house.

Mrs. Filmore died about ten months after Eddie's funeral and was buried at Cathedral Cemetery in the family plot with her husband and Eddie.

Upon graduation, Terry was offered and accepted a position with the AG's office in Harrisburg, working on Tommy's staff.

Phil, Stanley, Dan and Mike are healing.

Sean and Junior are optimistic about their teams for the upcoming season

The End

Please go to my website for more information about my Upstate Mysteries and a FREE short story. Here's the link.

https://upstatemystery.com/

Scroll down for more about the author and other novellas.

HIT AND RUN: IT LOOKED like a hit and run on a county road. However, Investigator Brad Petronella does not believe it. The evidence does not support it. Hi investigation uncover so much more!

https://books2read.com/u/b5val6

RIGHT TIME WRONG PLACE: A murder in an assisted living home. Who would want to kill this defenseless lady? Elton Hendricks, a transfer from the NYPD who with the help of familiar local characters, discovers the truth.

https://books2read.com/u/md7MWd

THE CARIBBEAN LAUNDRY: An independent accountant is murdered in his home. Detective Elton Hendricks investigates and a lucky find opens up a crime far beyond this quiet upstate town

https://books2read.com/u/mYZdlo

TWO MURDERS BY THE River: Two homicides within minutes of each other! Robbery? Revenge killing? Contract hit? The police have to solve this quickly, or the impact of this horrific crime on the town will be devastating.

Detectives Hendricks and Adams embark on an investigation that takes them far outside of upstate New York to another country.

Nobody will feel safe until the crime is solved.

https://books2read.com/u/4jAZ7X

I'M A RETIRED INTERNATIONAL Sales Director, having worked in the commercial and military flight simulation industry for over 30 years. I lived in Brussels (Belgium) and Bonn (Germany) for eight years and met my British wife in Brussels. Before my career in the flight simulation industry, I was an Armaments and Electronics Maintenance Officer in the USAF during the Viet Nam conflict. We have three children and seven grandchildren.

Since retirement I continue to chase an ever-elusive golf game.

Home is a small town in central New York State where the novellas are set.

I'm a volunteer mediator and Lemon Law arbitrator and this occasionally appears in the stories. An underlying theme in my novellas is people helping people. In spite of the difficulties and crime that may surround us, there is always hope in friendship and good neighbors.

This is my second novella and I plan on releasing a series of Brad Petronella cozy mysteries. Go to my website for information about my upcoming novellas, to contact me or a FREE short story. I won't use your information for any other purpose.

https://upstatemysteries.godaddysites.com/

Don't miss out!

Visit the website below and you can sign up to receive emails whenever fj donohue publishes a new book. There's no charge and no obligation.

https://books2read.com/r/B-A-CFSO-BDBPB

BOOKS2READ

Connecting independent readers to independent writers.

Also by fj donohue

Endwell Investigations
Full Circle
Vindication

Upstate Mystery
Hit and Run
Two Murders by the River
A Serial Killer Returns
Right Time Wrong Place
The Caribbean Laundry

Upstate Mystery #2
Closure

Upstate Mystery #7
The Snowbird Bank Robber

Watch for more at https://upstatemystery.com.